Someday We Will

A Book for
Grandparents and Grandchildren

by

Pam Webb

illustrated by

Wendy Leach

beaming books

MINNEAPOLIS

SOMEDAY

we'll take a walk in the park
and wave to the ducks paddling in the pond.

SOMEDAY

we'll draw chalk dinosaurs and butterflies along the front sidewalk.

SOMEDAY
we'll visit the zoo,
or maybe the museum . . .

Your choice!

SOMEDAY

we'll hike our bikes
up, up the hill

and then coast all the way down,
laughing into the wind.

SOMEDAY we'll have dessert first.

SOMEDAY

we'll swim all afternoon
and sit in the shade,

resting in the breeze.

SOMEDAY

we'll find a cozy nook
and share our favorite books.

SOMEDAY

we'll blow bubbles
big and small,

chasing them
as they float and burst and fall.

SOMEDAY

we'll fly our kites
until they drift up, up, up,

almost out of sight.

SOMEDAY we'll watch the sun set and applaud
the show of colors fading across the sky.

SOMEDAY

we'll watch movies on the couch,
snuggled together under a blanket

with a bowl of popcorn on our laps.

SOMEDAY we'll jump into the car,
laughing and singing songs

as we search
for our next adventure.

SOMEDAY . . .

SOMEDAY . . .

TO ZARA—FOR ALL OUR SOMEDAYS TO COME

26 25 24 23 22 21 20   1 2 3 4 5 6 7 8

ISBN: 978-1-5064-5400-9

Library of Congress Cataloging-in-Publication Data
Names: Webb, Pam, 1957- author. | Leach, Wendy, illustrator.
Title: Someday we will / by Pam Webb ; illustrated by Wendy Leach.
Description: Minneapolis, MN : Beaming Books, 2020. | Audience: Ages 3-8. |
    Summary: Grandparents and children anticipate their next visit by
    imagining all of the wonderful things they will do together, such as
    playing games, reading library books, and riding bicycles.
Identifiers: LCCN 2019034499 | ISBN 9781506454009 (hardcover)
Subjects: CYAC: Grandparent and child--Fiction.
Classification: LCC PZ7.1.W4179 Som 2020 | DDC [E]--dc23
LC record available at https://lccn.loc.gov/2019034499

VN0004589; 9781506454009; FEB2020

Beaming Books
510 Marquette Avenue
Minneapolis, MN 55402
Beamingbooks.com

ABOUT THE AUTHOR AND ILLUSTRATOR

PAM WEBB cultivated a love for stories in childhood trips to the library and began to dream of becoming a writer after encouragement from her fifth grade teacher. She has been a contributor to *Marvin Composes a Tea* and *Farmer Featherwit and the Rolling Pins*.

WENDY LEACH currently lives in Overland Park, Kansas, a suburb of Kansas City. Her favorite subjects to draw include cute kids and their pets, city landscapes, and lush garden spaces.